Bordaria
Difendere con Coraggio

Scholastic Canada Ltd.
604 King Street West, Toronto, Ontario M5V 1E1, Canada

Scholastic Inc.
557 Broadway, New York, NY 10012, USA

Scholastic Australia Pty Limited
PO Box 579, Gosford, NSW 2250, Australia

Scholastic New Zealand Limited
Private Bag 94407, Botany, Manukau 2163, New Zealand

Scholastic Children's Books
Euston House, 24 Eversholt Street, London NW1 1DB, UK

PÖP & FÏZZ

Text, design and illustration copyright © Lemonfizz Media, 2010.
Cover illustration by Britt Martin.
Internal illustrations by Lionel Portier, Melanie Matthews and James Hart.
First published by Pop & Fizz and Scholastic Australia in 2010.
Pop & Fizz is a partnership between Paddlepop Press and Lemonfizz Media.
www.paddlepoppress.com
This edition published under licence from Scholastic Australia Pty Limited
on behalf of Lemonfizz Media.

First published by Scholastic Australia in 2010.
This edition published by Scholastic Canada Ltd., 2011.

Library and Archives Canada Cataloguing in Publication

Park, Mac

Aquatan / Mac Park ; illustrations by Melanie Matthews, Lionel Portier and James Hart.

(Boy vs beast. Battle of the worlds)

ISBN 978-1-4431-0747-1

I. Matthews, Melanie, 1986- II. Portier, Lionel
III. Hart, James, 1981- IV. Title. V. Series: Park, Mac.

Boy vs beast. Battle of the worlds.

PZ7.P2213Aq 2011   j823'.92   C2010-907354-1

6 5 4 3 2 1   Printed in Canada 116   11 12 13 14 15

BOY vs BEAST

BATTLE OF THE WORLDS

AQUATAN

Mac Park

POP & FIZZ

SCHOLASTIC

Prologue

nce, mega-beast and man shared one world. But it did not last. The beasts wanted to rule the world. They started battles against man. After many bad battles between beast and man, the world was split in two. Man was given Earth. Mega-beasts were given Beastium.

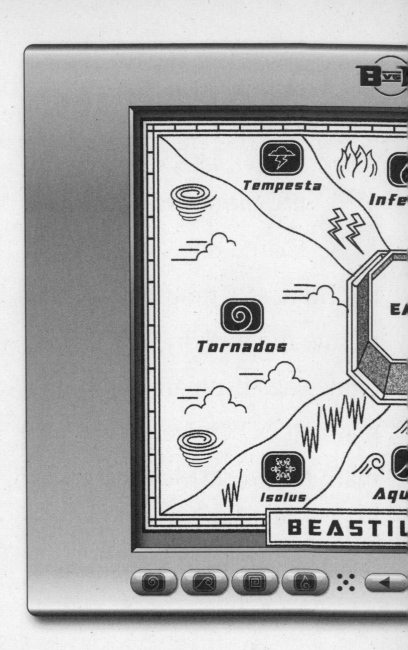

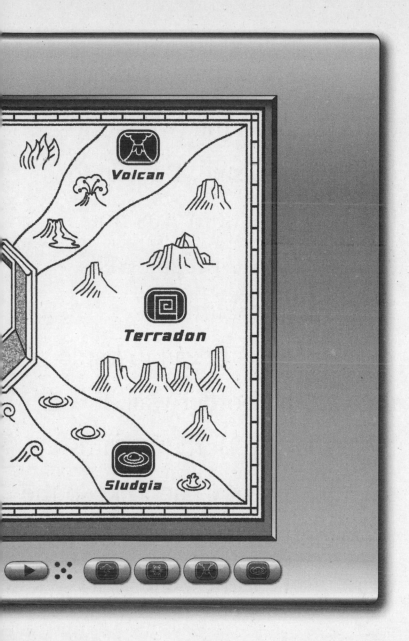

Volcan

Terradon

Sludgia

A border-wall was created. It closed the two worlds off. Man was safe. But not for long . . . Beastium was not enough for the mega-beasts. They wanted Earth.

The beasts began to battle through the border-wall. It was the job of the Border Guards to stop them. They had to keep the beasts in Beastium. Some battles were won. Some were lost.

Battles won by the beasts gave them more power. The beasts earned new battle attacks. Battles won by the Border Guards earned them upgrades. Their battle gear could do more.

Five boys now guard the border-wall. They are the Bordaria Border Guards. They are in training to become Border Masters like their dads.

The Bordaria Master Command

The Border Guards' dads and granddads are the Bordaria Master Command. The BMC helps the Border Guards during battle.

The Border Guards must learn. The safety of Earth depends on them.

The BMC rewards good Border Guard battling. Upgrades can be earned for sending beasts back into their lands. New battle gear can also be given to Border Guards who battle well.

If they do not battle well, the Border Guards will lose upgrades and points. Then they will not be given new and better gear.

Kai Masters is a Border Guard in training. His work is top secret. He must protect Earth. The BMC watches Kai closely. Kai must not fail.

Let the battles commence!

Chapter 1

Kai Masters was at home. He was playing a computer game. It was called *Wild Water ride*. The game was a speedboat race. It was hard. Kai's boat was just out in front.

Kai was close to the end of the race.

Suddenly Kai's dog, BC3, barked.

Woof! Woof!

The dog was at the back door. And its tail was wagging.

BC3 was Kai's buddy. Kai called him BC for short. But BC was not just any dog. He was a dogbot. And he was made for beast battling. BC could see in front of himself. He could see behind himself, too.

ROBOTIC CANINE BC3

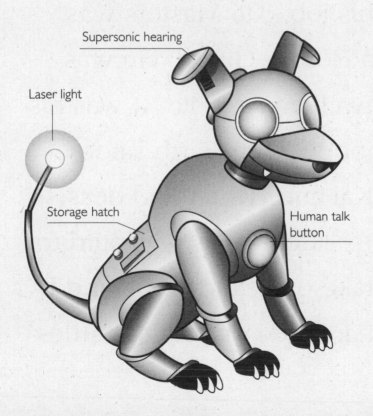

Supersonic hearing

Laser light

Storage hatch

Human talk button

And BC's tail wagged when there was trouble.

BC was a gift from the BMC. He helped Kai do his job. Kai Masters was a Border Guard. He was twelve years old. It was his job to keep Earth safe. Kai and BC battled beasts.

These beasts wanted to take over Earth. Kai and BC had been on lots of battles to stop the beasts. They were good at battling. But they were still learning.

Kai's dad was once a Border Guard. Then he became a Border Master. He was part of the Bordaria Master Command now.

The BMC helped Kai learn. Kai wanted to become a Border Master one day, too. Just like his dad.

"Stop it, BC," said Kai.
"Be good."

But BC barked louder and louder.

Woof! Woof!

He wants to go out badly, thought Kai. *And his tail is wagging. That can't be good.*

Kai looked out the

lighthouse's big window.

The lighthouse was Kai's home. It looked old from the outside. But the inside was very new. It had secret rooms where Kai kept his battle gear.

Kai looked at the beach. "What are all those things on the sand?" he asked.

BC barked again. "Okay," said Kai. "I'll let you talk."

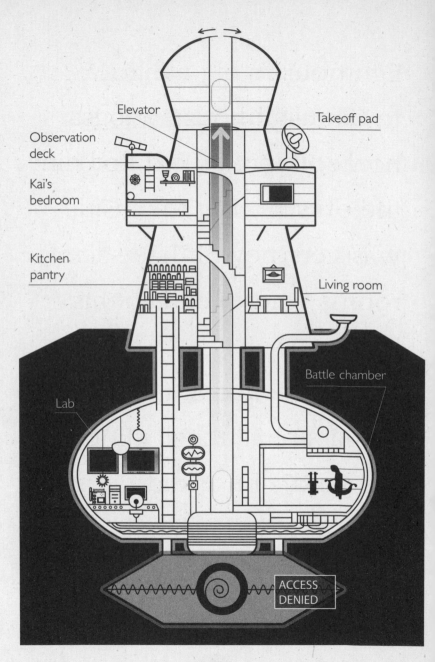

Observation deck

Elevator

Takeoff pad

Kai's bedroom

Kitchen pantry

Living room

Battle chamber

Lab

ACCESS DENIED

20

Sometimes Kai liked BC to be just like other dogs. And sometimes he liked him to be a dogbot. BC was great in battles.

Kai hit the button so that BC could talk.

"A bad smell is coming from the beach," said BC.

"I can't smell anything," said Kai. "But you can pick out scents very well."

"Trouble on the beach," said BC.

"We'd better go and look then," said Kai. "Good dog, BC."

Chapter 2

There was no one on the beach. Kai looked at the fish on the sand. They were just bones. "Where are their bodies?" asked Kai. "And what's that green stuff?"

"Green slime," said BC. "Let's take some home," said Kai.

Kai took his orbix from his pocket. It was a small computer. It had lots of good stuff on it.

The BMC used it to talk with Kai. And they sent Kai's upgrades on it. It could also hold things Kai shouldn't touch.

Kai hit a button on the orb.
The screen flashed.

Get sample

A flat metal rod came out
from the orb. The rod went
along the fish bones. It picked
up some green slime.

Then the rod went back inside the orb. "I bet this stuff is from Beastium," said Kai. "We can test it in the lab."

Kai and BC ran back up to the lighthouse. They went into the kitchen. Kai pushed a button under the pantry shelf.

The back wall of the pantry began to move.

It slid open. A secret ladder
was behind the wall.
Kai and BC went down
the ladder into the lab.
It had lots of tools in it.
Kai used them to look at
things that might have
come from Beastium.

Kai turned on the sample
tester. He put the slime
into it. Then he hit the test
button on the computer.

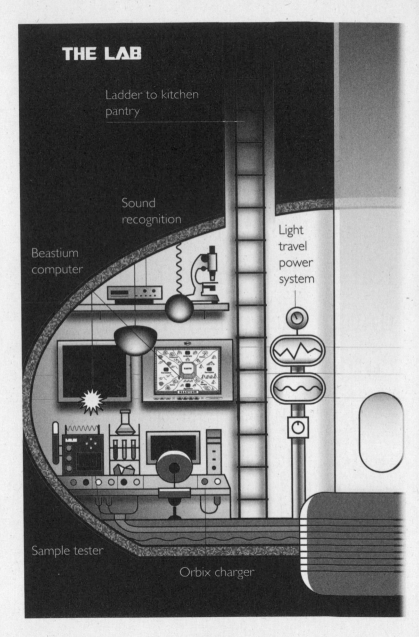

THE LAB

Ladder to kitchen pantry

Sound recognition

Beastium computer

Light travel power system

Sample tester

Orbix charger

The screen flashed.

The rock land and the water land, thought Kai. *Which one? The slime has a lot of water in it. But there's only a bit of rock and dust.*

Kai went for the water land. He hit the Aquatan button. A card popped up.

Then the computer flashed
again.

"This will be our first
water battle. We'll need some
underwater gear. We'd better
get ready for battle," said Kai.

Chapter 3

Kai took out his Border
Guard Card. It looked like
a student card. He put the
card into his computer.
Then there was a very loud
noise.

CLUNK! BANG!

Whiiiir! BANG!

Four big bricks in the wall behind Kai began to move. They made a hole in the wall. Kai went through the hole into the room.

It had three walls with battle gear on them.

A screen was over the last wall. *I can't have stuff from that wall,* thought Kai. *It's still locked. I need to win more battles.*

On the second wall was
a heat laser. Kai read its tag.
"This can dry up water.
We want this, BC," said Kai.

Kai went to take it.
He heard a noise like locks
closing. Then he heard

CLUNK!

GRRRR **CLUNK!**

Then a computer voice said,

"Not yet!"

"When will the BMC let

me have things from these other walls?" asked Kai. "Oh well."

Kai looked at the things on the first wall. "Let's take this, BC," said Kai.

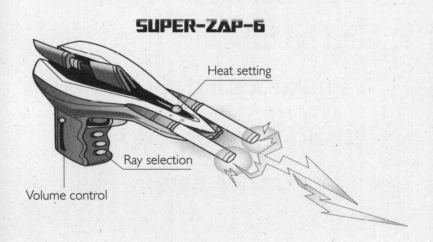

SUPER-ZAP-6

Heat setting

Ray selection

Volume control

"This thing can zap stuff and heat up water. Maybe this could be handy," said Kai.

"We can only have one more thing from here," said BC.

"Yes," said Kai. "I think it should be this."

"What does it do?" asked BC.

"It shoots a torpedo that goes fast under water," said Kai.

TORPEDO CROSSBOW

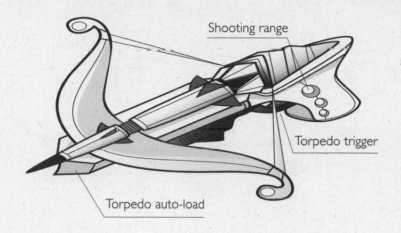

Shooting range

Torpedo trigger

Torpedo auto-load

Kai and BC went back
into the lab. Then Kai
picked up his hoverboard.
It had jets and could go at
fast speeds.

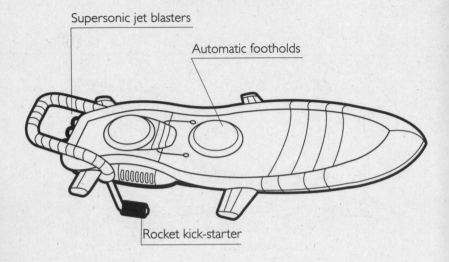

HOVERBOARD

Supersonic jet blasters

Automatic footholds

Rocket kick-starter

"And I think we should take this," said Kai.

Kai and BC went into the elevator. It took them to the takeoff pad. Kai pushed the

code for Aquatan on his orb.
The elevator went up to the
top floor. When Kai got out,
he was in full battle gear.

"The BMC has given us
underwater tanks!" said Kai.

Just then Kai's orb beeped.

Clothes
water and rot
moss proof

"What's rot moss?" asked Kai.

"The green slime maybe," said BC.

"It doesn't sound like fun stuff," said Kai. "Time to go."

Kai hit the light button on the orb. The roof of the lighthouse opened.

The takeoff pad lit up with light. The light went up into the sky.

It took Kai and BC with it
to the water land.

Chapter 4

Kai hit the water with a splash. BC came right behind him. Kai hit the button on his orb for flippers. Flippers popped out from Kai's shoes. BC got four flippers, too.

Then Kai set his hoverboard to go up above the water.

It went up out of the water.
"It can wait for us up there,"
said Kai.

Kai and BC went down
to the sea floor. There was
glowing green slime all over
the place.

Rot moss, thought Kai.
He looked it up on his orb.

Toxic rot
moss eats skin

"Great!" said Kai. "It eats skin. And we have to go right through it."

"I'll go first and find the best way," said BC. "Slime can't eat my body. I'm a robot."

Kai moved slowly behind
BC. He had to watch out.
His face and hands could be
eaten by the slime.

They made it to a clear
space. Kai looked up. They
were in very deep water.
But there was no slime.
"I'm glad that's over,"
said Kai. Just then his orb
flashed. "Hey, we got some
upgrades, BC."

"Our underwater packs have jets now. And I can see much better with my goggles. Good work getting us through that slime," said Kai.

Suddenly BC's tail started wagging. "What now?" asked Kai. "A wagging tail isn't good. It's always something bad!"

And then he saw them.

Jelly-fish. Before they knew it they both had jelly-fish all over them. Kai had to do something fast. The jelly-fish had long stingers. And they were going around Kai's arms.

"I can't move and I can't see," said Kai. His goggles had jelly-fish on them as well. Jelly-fish with stingers and drills!

"Drills are starting," said BC. "They will drill into your bones and my metal body."

Kai could hear them. The noise was getting louder.

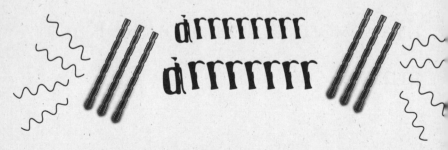

Kai got one hand free.
He pulled out the Super-
Zap-6. He hit a button.
The Super-Zap-6 shook.
But that was all.

Kai looked at BC.
BC was biting and pulling at
the jelly-fish. *I have to stop
this,* thought Kai. He tried
another button. A bad noise
filled the sea.

SCREEEEECH! SCREEEECH!!

Suddenly the jelly-fish started to shake. Their bodies shook and shook until they fell to bits. Little bits of jelly-fish were everywhere in the water.

"Are you okay, BC?" asked Kai.

"Okay," said BC. "Just! But I can hear something else now."

Chapter 5

Kai stood on the sea floor and listened. "What's the noise, BC?" asked Kai. And then he heard it.

It was coming from in the water.

AWWWWOOOO

Kai turned the button on his goggles to full strength. He looked at what was making the noise. "It's only a little one," said Kai. "This will be an easy battle."

The little beast slid across the sea floor. It moved toward Kai and BC like a snake. It kicked up slime with every move it made.

Kai swam around trying to miss the slime. But that was when the little beast made its move. It was around BC in a second.

In no time it had the dog in a crush-attack.

BC was getting crushed. Kai got out his bow. But he couldn't shoot.

The little beast was all over BC. *I have to hit the beast and not BC,* thought Kai. *But how?* Kai held his breath. 1, 2, 3. The bow went off.

BOOM!

The torpedo shot through the water. Everything went quiet. Kai didn't want to look. The water stopped moving and there was BC. He was standing on the sea floor. And he was shaking. The little beast was gone.

"Are you okay?" asked Kai.

"Yes. But my underwater pack got blown up. And I am shaking," said BC.

"Everything's shaking, BC," said Kai. Kai used the orb to call the hoverboard. "Jump on and wait for me up top."

Kai didn't know why everything was shaking. But he didn't think it was good.

Chapter 6

BC rode up and out of the water. Kai looked at the sea floor. It was really shaking. *What's going on?* he thought. Kai looked all around him.

He could see strange blobs. They were falling into a nest of slime.

Kai saw glowing green eggs in the nest.

Kai watched as the water around the nest began to turn. It turned around and around. The eggs and slime came together in the water. They were turning around with the water.

The water was so strong it was pulling Kai into it. Kai turned his underwater

pack to top speed. He pushed
away from the turning water.

Then the water stopped.
Everything went still.
Kai couldn't see what was
going on. Then a big sucking
sound began.

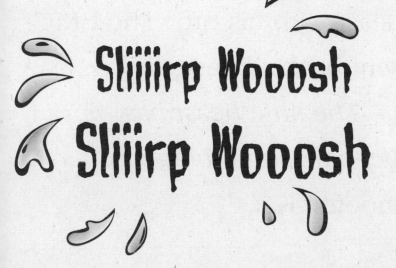

Sliiiirp Wooosh
Sliiiirp Wooosh

The water was being sucked out from under Kai. It was very strong. And the thing doing it was huge and ugly. It was a beast. And it was right in front of Kai.

Kai took a photo of the beast with his orb. The BMC sent back a beast card.

The little beast has become something else, thought Kai.

BEAST I.D.

SERPEGATAN
Watch out for the wave attack

Strength ★★★⯪☆

Attack Power ★★★★☆

Speed ★★★☆☆

Kai went above the water.
He jumped on the hoverboard
with BC. "The beast is about
to attack," said Kai.

They hit the bottom and the water froze around them.

We're trapped in ice.

It's working.

I'll use the Super-Zap-6 to melt it. Turn on the hoverboard jets.

We're free! Now let's go get this beast.

hey went back to the water and. Then the beast attacked hem with water bombs.

Those water bombs will send us flying. Watch out!

water bomb hit Kai ight in the chest. SSPLAAAASHH!

I'll get you.

Aaaaaghhh

The beast was very mad now. It turned the sea into a huge wall of water.

There's a crystal falling from the sky.

I'll catch it. Maybe it was sent to us by the BMC.

The huge wall of water threw Kai and BC back into the ice land.

WHPLAACK!

Oooowwww...

Kai came off the board and fell onto the ice.

The beast left. He knew that soon Kai would be frozen there forever.

Chapter 7

Kai hit the ice hard. He had slime on his hands and face. It made him fall asleep.

BC had been thrown to the other side of the ice. But he was still on the hoverboard. BC went over to Kai. BC took the crystal from his hatch.

He rubbed the crystal over the slime on Kai's skin. It worked. The slime went away. Kai's skin was all right again. And he was starting to wake up.

"The crystal," said BC. "It gets rid of slime. And it can make ice."

"How do you know?" asked Kai.

"Data in storage hatch," said BC.

"What?" asked Kai.

But then the ice began to rock and shake.

The beast was on top of them. It had Kai in its tail.

BC was in its suckers.

They were stuck in a crush-attack. "Use bow to shoot the crystal," said BC. "It will save us."

"Are you nuts?" yelled Kai.

Kai looked at BC. The beast had its mouth open. It was pulling BC toward it. BC growled loudly. He tried to break free, but he couldn't.

I have to trust BC,
thought Kai. "Okay," Kai said
to BC. "Throw the crystal
up into the air." BC did.
The crystal went up into the
sky. Kai fired the torpedo.

The torpedo hit the
crystal in its middle.

The crystal burst open.
It broke into lots of pieces.
The pieces were made of
ice. They fell down onto
the beast. And they kept
coming. The beast let out a
big noise.

EEEEEOOOOWWWW

It had bits of sharp ice all
over it.

More ice fell from where the crystal had broken open. It didn't stop.

The beast's tail suddenly let go of Kai. Kai came down hard on the ice. BC fell down on the ice after him. Then Kai heard a funny sound.

Creak Crackle
Creak Crackle

"Look," said BC. "The beast is in ice. It can't get out."

Kai looked.

The beast was frozen in ice. Kai and BC had won. Their battle was over.

"We did it," said Kai. "Earth is safe again."

"The ice won't melt and set it free?" asked BC.

"No," said Kai. "This is an ice land. Everything is always frozen here." Or so Kai thought.

Chapter 8

Kai took out his orb.

The screen flashed.

"You got an upgrade, BC. That's how you knew about the crystal," said Kai.

"Come on then, home time," said Kai. He pushed the button for home on the orb.

A bright light came down from above. It picked up Kai and BC. In a second they were back in the lighthouse. Earth was safe again.

For now.

SERPEGATAN

This beast needs a melt down

Battle Plays	★★
New Attacks	★★★
Energy	⯪

Kai Masters

Kai put this beast on ice

Battle Plays ★★★ ☆ ☆

Upgrades ★★★ ☆ ☆

Bonus Items ★ ☆ ☆ ☆ ☆

www.boyvsbeast.com

web mode

BATTLE OF THE WORLDS

Have you read them all?